RAINBOW
magic ®
The Fun Day Fairies

For Charlotte Tilley,
with lots of love and
fairy magic

Special thanks to
Sue Mongredien

ORCHARD BOOKS
338 Euston Road, London NW1 3BH
Orchard Books Australia
Hachette Children's Books
Level 17/207 Kent Street, Sydney, NSW 2000
A Paperback Original

First published in Great Britain in 2006
Rainbow Magic is a registered trademark of Working Partners Limited.
Series created by Working Partners Limited, London W6 OQT

Text © Working Partners Limited 2006
Illustrations © Georgie Ripper 2006
The right of Georgie Ripper to be identified as the illustrator
of this work has been asserted by her in accordance
with the Copyright, Designs and Patents Act, 1988.
A CIP catalogue record for this book is available
from the British Library.

ISBN 1 84616 189 4
1 3 5 7 9 10 8 6 4 2

Printed in Great Britain

Tallulah
the Tuesday Fairy

by Daisy Meadows

illustrated by Georgie Ripper

ORCHARD BOOKS

www.rainbowmagic.co.uk

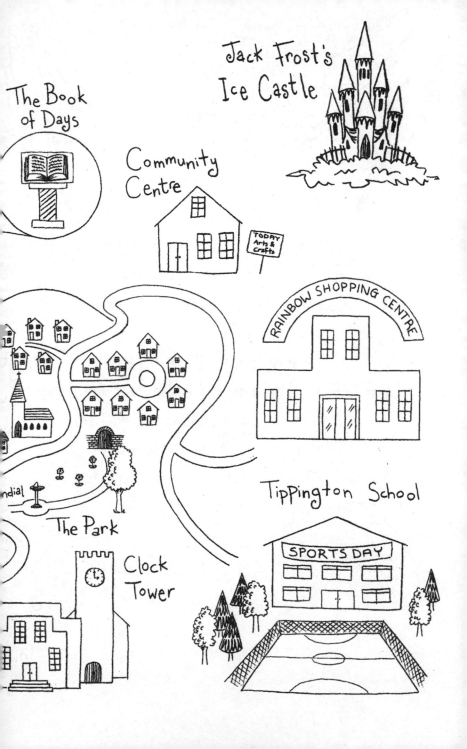

The Book
of Days

Jack Frost's
Ice Castle

Community
Centre

TODAY
Arts &
Crafts

RAINBOW SHOPPING CENTRE

Tippington School

SPORTS DAY

ndial

The Park

Clock
Tower

Icy wind now fiercely blow!
To the Time Tower I must go.
Goblin servants follow me
And steal the Fun Day Flags I need.

I know there will be no fun,
For fairies or humans once the flags are gone.
So, storm winds, take me where I say.
My plan for chaos starts today!

Contents

Sports Day Sparkle

"Come on, Rachel! You can do it!"
Kirsty Tate cheered as she watched
her friend race on the sunny playing
field. Today was Tippington Schools'
Sports Day. The three local schools had
come together to compete in all sorts of
different events. As Kirsty was staying
with her best friend, Rachel Walker,

in Tippington for the half-term holiday, she'd come along to watch.

The 100-metre sprint was the last race of the morning, and Rachel was doing really well. She was neck and neck with one other girl as they approached the finishing line.

"Come on, Rachel, keep going!"
yelled Kirsty excitedly. The two runners
were so close it was impossible to guess
who was going to win. Then, at the
very last moment, with a final burst of
speed, Rachel surged past the other girl,
and crossed the finishing line.

"Yay! Rachel wins!"
Kirsty cheered, jumping
up and down. She
beamed at some of
the other children
who'd watched the
race, but they all
looked unhappy.
*They must have
wanted the other girl to
win really badly*, Kirsty
thought to herself in surprise.

Rachel came over a few moments later, pink-cheeked and smiling. "Phew – that was a close one," she panted.

"You did brilliantly," Kirsty smiled. "What an exciting race!"

"Well, I thought so," Rachel said. "But have you noticed how everyone else seems really fed up?"

Kirsty looked around. It was true. A girl nearby was scuffing the grass with her foot and moaning to her dad that she was too cold, and one of the bigger boys was saying that he was hungry. Even some of the teachers seemed bored.

A thought struck both
girls at exactly the
same time. "It must be
because the Tuesday
Fun Flag is missing,"
Kirsty said in a low voice.

"Just what I was about to say,"
Rachel agreed. "That's why nobody's
having much fun today!"

Rachel and Kirsty shared an exciting
secret: they were on a mission to help
the fairies! Jack Frost had stolen the
seven Fun Day Flags, used by the Fun
Day Fairies to bring fun to everyone in
Fairyland and in the human world. But
once the flags were in Jack Frost's ice
castle, his goblin servants started having
all sorts of fun, playing lots of cheeky
tricks on Jack Frost!

Fed up with the goblins' mischief, Jack Frost sent a breeze to blow the flags into the human world. Little did he know that his goblins missed their fun and games so much, they had sneaked away to find the flags again.

"We'll have to look out for Tallulah the Tuesday Fairy," Rachel said, glancing around hopefully. "The sooner we can find the Tuesday Fun Flag so that Tallulah can work her magic, the better for everyone!"

Just then an announcement came over the tannoy. "The morning's races are now finished. Please make your way to the assembly hall, where there will be a presentation of prizes before lunch. Thank you."

The Sports Day was taking place at Rachel's school, so she led Kirsty inside to the hall. A stage had been set up along one wall for the first, second and third prize winners to receive their medals.

"I'll meet you afterwards, OK?" Rachel said, joining the group of winners waiting to collect their prizes.

"OK," Kirsty agreed, going to sit at the back of the hall to watch. As she took her seat, she noticed that a table had been set up behind her, at the very back of the room, with a big, impressive golden cup on it. *That must be the trophy for the school*  *that wins the most events*, she guessed.

A woman in a smart plum-coloured suit came and stood on the stage. "Good morning," she said. "I'm Jennie Bailey, Tippington's councillor, and I'm delighted to be here to award some medals to you today."

As the councillor went on speaking, Kirsty heard a tiny sound and turned round. To her surprise the golden trophy was glittering extra brightly. Nobody else had noticed because everyone was sitting with their backs to the trophy table. Then the trophy lid rattled, and a stream of turquoise sparkles came drifting out from inside the cup.

Rhyming Clue

Kirsty recognized fairy magic when she
saw it! But how could she go over and
investigate without everyone noticing
and wondering what she was doing?
Luckily, at that moment, everybody else
in the audience started clapping loudly
for the children who'd won prizes, so
Kirsty quietly slipped out of her seat

and over to the trophy. Very
carefully, she reached out, lifted the
lid and peeped inside. And there,
zooming around the inside of the cup,
was a tiny fairy!

Kirsty and Rachel had met all the
Fun Day Fairies yesterday, and Kirsty
recognised Tallulah the Tuesday Fairy
at once. "Hello, Tallulah!" she
whispered, smiling.

Tallulah beamed thankfully as she
saw Kirsty's face, and fluttered
quickly out of the trophy. She had
long, brown curly hair, which was
swept up into a high ponytail, and
she wore a cropped blue jacket and
blue trousers, with a pretty flower
necklace around her neck.
"Thanks for letting
me out," she replied
in a whisper.
"I came here to
find the Tuesday
Fun Flag, but
I didn't mean to get
stuck in that trophy!"

"Well, you've turned up at just
the right time," Kirsty whispered
back. "Nobody is having fun here."

Tallulah opened her mouth to reply, but then got distracted by the councillor's words.

"I'm sorry to announce," the councillor was saying, "that the medals and certificates for our winners have been mislaid. The winners will receive tokens instead for the time being, and we will break for lunch now. I'm sure that the proper prizes will turn up soon."

There were a few mumbles of disappointment, and then the audience started leaving the hall. Tallulah promptly dived into Kirsty's pocket out of sight.

"I was looking forward to my prize,"
Kirsty heard one little girl saying sadly.
"This Sports Day is no fun at all."

Rachel came over to Kirsty and
Tallulah, looking
rather downcast.
She brightened
when she saw the
little fairy peeping
out of Kirsty's
pocket, though.
"Oh, Tallulah, thank
goodness you're here!" she said.
"Let's all go and find a quiet spot to
talk. We really need to find your flag."

The three of them left the hall and
Rachel led them to an empty corridor.
"While everyone's getting lunch, we
should be safe here," she said.

"Tallulah, do you have any clues from the Book of Days?"

Rachel and Kirsty had learned yesterday that every morning in Fairyland, Francis, the Royal Time Guard, consulted a large book to check which day it was. Then he ran that day's flag up the flagpole. Yesterday, with all the Fun Day Flags

missing, a riddle had appeared in the
Book of Days instead, and it had
helped the girls find Megan the
Monday Fairy's flag.

"Francis looked in the book this
morning and there was a new poem in
it," Tallulah said. "It goes like this:

In the air, not on the ground
At Sports Day, flags are all around.
Check the coloured decorations
For Tuesday Fun Flag celebrations!"

"Check the coloured decorations..."
Rachel repeated thoughtfully.

"That's right," Tallulah said. "The
Tuesday Fun Flag is turquoise and
sparkly, so—"

But, before she could say another
word, a cupboard door
behind the girls
suddenly burst
open. Kirsty and
Rachel jumped
out of the way
as a tangle of
mops and brooms
crashed to the
ground, and out
hopped two grinning
goblins who had clearly
been listening to every word!

"Thanks for telling us the poem," one of them cackled gloatingly.

"Yes, now we know where to look for the flag," the other one chortled. "And we'll be taking it home with us!" And, with that, the goblins ran away down the corridor, chuckling gleefully.

Goblins Have a Head Start

"Oh, no!" Kirsty cried. "Where are they going?"

"Don't worry," Rachel said. "It's OK. I think I've worked out the riddle. The clue is in the first line."

Tallulah looked around hurriedly. "Don't say another word," she warned, "in case there are any other sneaky goblins nearby.

29

Just take us to where you think the flag might be."

"OK," Rachel said. "This way!"

Tallulah quickly waved her wand so that all the mops and brooms jumped back into the cupboard and the door swung shut in a burst of turquoise glitter. Then Rachel led Kirsty and Tallulah back towards the sports field. Luckily, it was quite empty now, as everybody had gone to get lunch, so Tallulah could fly in the open air without anyone seeing her. Kirsty pulled a couple of apples from her bag, and the girls munched as they walked.

When they reached the field, Rachel pointed up at the strings of coloured flags that fluttered in the breeze.

"The clue said the flag would be in the air, not on the ground, didn't it?" she said. "So I think it must be somewhere in this bunting!"

"Brilliant!" said Tallulah, clapping her hands in delight. But then she looked around and a determined gleam appeared in her eye. "There are lots of turquoise flags, though, and I can't tell which is mine from here. We'll have to look at each of them in turn to find the Tuesday flag."

Kirsty gazed down the length of the sports field. The bunting was strung

between poles marking out a large
rectangular shape on the grass where
the races were being run. The girls and
Tallulah were standing near the starting
line at one corner of the rectangle.
Strings of bunting stretched away from
them in two different directions. "I'll
start looking along this side," Kirsty
said, pointing to the line of flags on
her right.

"And I'll check the flags above the
starting line," Rachel said,
turning to her left.
"Then I'll fly
across to the other
side of the field
and look at the
bunting above
the finishing line,"
Tallulah said,
fluttering away quickly.

Kirsty began walking along checking
all the turquoise flags on her line of
bunting. There were triangular flags in
white, red, orange, yellow and
turquoise and there were hundreds of
them, dancing merrily in the breeze.
As she walked, she looked carefully at
all the turquoise flags, hoping to see

a telltale sparkle or two of fairy magic,
but there was no sign of the Tuesday
Fun Flag.

She glanced along the line of bunting
ahead to see how far she had to go,
and at that very moment she spotted
the sunlight glinting off a particularly
twinkly-looking turquoise flag at the
other end of the string. It was so
sparkly and bright, she felt sure it
must be the Tuesday Fun Flag.

"Over here!" she called to Rachel and
Tallulah, pointing at the flag. Then she
looked back at the bunting and her
smile vanished at once, for two goblins
had darted out from behind a tree, and
had seen where she was pointing!

"Oh, no," Kirsty cried, breaking into
a run. But the goblins were much
nearer to the flag, and before Kirsty
could get to it, they'd reached it with
a cheer of triumph.

"Don't worry, they're not tall enough to get it down," Rachel called out as she ran over. The goblins were far too short to be able to grab the flag, even if they stood on tiptoes.

"That's what you think!" one of the goblins sneered. He crouched down with his hands together, making a step for the other goblin. The second goblin

put his foot on the 'step', and his friend
boosted him up into the air. As he flew
upwards, the goblin reached out and
grabbed the flag firmly in his gnarly
green fingers. He stuck out his tongue
at the girls.

"What were you saying about us not being able to reach it?" he taunted gleefully. "Well, we just did, and now this flag means lots of Tuesday fun for us goblins!"

Girls Get Crafty

The goblin tugged at the flag with a grin on his face, but then his grin vanished. To his dismay, the flag wouldn't budge.

Kirsty held her breath, hoping that the flag was stuck tight to the bunting and that the goblin wouldn't be able to pull it free, but the triangular turquoise

flag suddenly came loose from the
string. As it did so, it unfolded to its
usual rectangular shape in the goblin's
hand. Kirsty could see the distinctive
sun pattern marked out on it in
turquoise glitter.

"Got it!" the goblin roared in
triumph, as he dropped to the ground.

"Run!" shouted the other goblin, haring across the field away from the girls and Tallulah.

"After them!" called Rachel, racing off in pursuit.

Kirsty was close behind. "Come back with that flag!" she yelled.

But the goblins didn't stop. They ran the length of the field and then dived into a marquee tent that had been set up in case of rain.

The girls and Tallulah followed
them inside and looked
around. There were mats
stacked up for the high
jump, sacks for the
sack race, hula
hoops, hurdles,
cones and all sorts
of other equipment
needed for Sports
Day, but there
was no sign of
any green goblins.

"There are loads
of good hiding places
in here, worst luck,"
Rachel murmured to her
friends. "We'd better get
searching for those goblins!"

Kirsty checked around the piles of mats but the goblins weren't hiding behind them. Rachel looked behind the rack of hula hoops, but there were no goblins there either. Tallulah waved her wand over a large crate of tennis balls, and with a stream of turquoise sparkles, all the balls bounced out in neat formation. "No goblins in there," she said, fluttering over the empty crate and waved her wand a second time.

Instantly, the tennis balls bounced
back into the crate,
lining themselves
up tidily.
Then, Rachel
went over to
a pile of sacks.
As she drew
closer, she saw
that there were
two sacks which
were upside-down,
and poking out the bottom of each one
was a pair of big green goblin feet.
Then she noticed that there was even
a corner of the twinkly turquoise flag
poking out of one sack, too! The
goblins had clearly put empty sacks
over their heads in an effort to hide.

Without a word, Rachel beckoned Kirsty and Tallulah over and pointed at what she'd seen. Then she drew them behind a pile of hurdles so that they could whisper together.

"We've got to think up a really good way to get those goblins out of there," Rachel said.

"Yes — and a way to get the flag to us!" Kirsty agreed in a low voice. She cast about the tent, looking for inspiration.

"Maybe we could tickle the goblin holding the flag until he lets go," Rachel suggested in a whisper. "You know how much goblins hate being tickled."

Tallulah looked doubtful. "Yes, but the flag is already in the sack with the goblin," she pointed out. "He might just pull it further inside to keep it safe."

Rachel and Tallulah looked at Kirsty hopefully. Rachel could see that her friend was frowning in thought. After a few moments, she said, "I think I've got an idea." She grinned at Rachel and Tallulah. "And it just might work!"

Three-legged Fun

"The goblins are standing right next to each other, so let's give them their very own three-legged race," Kirsty giggled, pulling a skipping rope out of a crate. "Tallulah, could you magic this rope to tie one goblin's right leg to the other goblin's left leg?" she whispered with a grin.

Rachel clapped a hand over her mouth to stop herself from laughing out loud at the idea. Tallulah was smiling, too, as she waved her wand in the air. A moment later the skipping rope flew obediently over to the goblins. In a turquoise blur of fairy sparkles, it wound itself around the left leg of the first goblin and the right leg of the second goblin, before tying itself tightly in a knot. The rope paused and then added a loopy bow, with a final burst of bright sparkles.

Tallulah chuckled softly. "They won't be able to run very far with my flag now," she said, her eyes sparkling with merriment.

"Now I'll grab the flag!" whispered Rachel.

She tiptoed over to the sack with the Fun Day Flag sticking out of it. Very quietly, she reached out, grasped the shimmering turquoise fabric, and yanked it sharply. She must have caught the goblin by surprise because the flag immediately came free.

"Hey!" the goblin yelled. "Who did that? Who pinched the flag? Was it you?"

"Me? No!" the other goblin replied. "It must be those pesky girls. Quick, we've got to get out of the sacks!"

Rachel ran back to the others as the two goblins threw their sacks off and tried to race after the girls, not realising that their legs were tied together.

"Whoa!" the first one yelled as he was pulled over by the second. "What happened?"

The second goblin was trying to get back on his feet, but he couldn't stand up. Then he noticed the skipping rope around his leg. "They've played a trick on us!" he moaned. "We're tied together!" His fingers scrabbled at the knots, but they wouldn't come undone for they were fastened tightly with fairy magic.

After a moment, he gave up and the two goblins tried to stand up together and walk. Rachel and Kirsty couldn't resist watching as they swayed and wobbled and then fell over again. It was so funny!

"Hey – stop pushing me!" the first goblin moaned.

"You're pushing me, you idiot!" the second goblin snapped. "And now those girls have got our flag!"

"Sorry," Tallulah said. "It's my flag, and if you two try and get it again, I'll tell Jack Frost you were trying to sneak it back into his ice castle!" She grinned cheekily. "Don't worry, though. As soon as my flag's back in Fairyland where it belongs, the rope will magically undo itself."

The goblins' shoulders slumped at her words. They knew they were beaten, so they sighed and stumbled off jerkily, still grumbling about being tied together with the skipping rope.

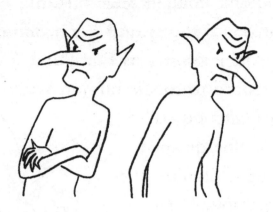

"Here you are, Tallulah" Rachel said, handing the sparkly flag to the little fairy.

"Thank you," Tallulah said
happily, as she waved her wand to
shrink the flag to its Fairyland size. In
order to fit into the human world, the
flag had magically
grown bigger.
"Now I'd better
zoom back to
Fairyland, to
recharge my
wand with
Tuesday magic."
The girls knew
that the Fun Day
Magic needed to be
collected by the Fun Day Fairies
in a special way. Tallulah would
have to return to Fairyland and give
the Tuesday Fun Flag to Francis,

who would run it to the top of the
flagpole on the Time Tower. Then
Tallulah would stand in the courtyard
below and hold up her wand. When
the sun's rays struck the glittery pattern
on the Fun Day Flag, a stream of

Tuesday magic would be reflected from the flag down to Tallulah's wand.

"I won't be long," Tallulah said. "And when I get back, I'll set to work to make this Sports Day full of fun!"

Tuesday Fun For Everyone!

"Great," Rachel said happily. "See you soon!"

They waved goodbye to the smiling fairy as she disappeared in a flurry of bright fairy dust. And then, seconds later, a teacher walked into the tent, looking rather surprised to see the girls standing there.

"Hello," the teacher said in a puzzled voice. Then her face cleared. "Oh, are you here to help me get the sacks for the sack race?"

"Um…yes," Rachel said quickly, feeling relieved that there weren't still two sneaky goblins in the sacks!

"Great," the teacher replied, picking up a stack of the sacks. "If you could each take another pile of these, that would be really helpful. The afternoon events are due to start in a few minutes."

"No problem," Kirsty said politely, picking up a pile of sacks.

"I hope Tallulah comes back soon," Rachel whispered to Kirsty, as they left the tent. "Look at everyone's faces!"

Kirsty looked around as she and
Rachel carried their sacks across the
field and set them down by the starting
line. She could see that lots of children
were now drifting back to the field
after lunch, but they all looked
rather miserable.

At that moment, an announcement came over the tannoy. "The sack race is about to begin. Would all competitors please come to the starting line to take their places?"

While the morning's events had been for the pupils of the three schools only, the afternoon's activities were fun races and games for anyone to enter, including guests, parents and teachers. Kirsty and Rachel were looking forward to racing together in lots of events, including the sack race.

They watched as a crowd of boys and girls came to the starting line, all looking gloomy and unenthusiastic about the race.

"My sack feels really scratchy," one girl grumbled as she stepped into it.

"I wish I hadn't entered this race," her friend muttered.

Kirsty and Rachel stepped into their own sacks, looking around for a sign of Tallulah. "I hope everything's all right," Kirsty whispered to Rachel. "What if something's happened to Tallulah and her flag?"

"On your marks…get set…" a
teacher called, holding up a starting
gun. "GO!" As she fired the gun, there
was a loud bang and turquoise glitter
showered all over the sack racers! The
teacher looked surprised, but Kirsty and
Rachel grinned at one another.

"Fairy dust!" giggled Kirsty.

"Tallulah must be back with her Fun
Day Magic!" Rachel said happily.
"She's just in time!"

"Oops – the race has
started!" Kirsty laughed,
suddenly remembering
that they were
supposed to be
bouncing along in
their sacks. "Come
on, Rachel!"

There were
squeals of laughter
from the other
children, and breathless
shouts as they all jumped
along in their sacks, trying
to reach the finishing line first.

"This is such fun!" Rachel heard

70

one boy shout, with a big grin on his face. "Can't catch me!" a girl yelled, in fits of giggles. Kirsty and Rachel couldn't help laughing too. "Fairy magic is amazing!" Kirsty said as they jumped along together. "Suddenly, everyone is having fun again!" "And it's all thanks to Tallulah," Rachel laughed. "Hurrah for Fun Day Magic!" A little girl won the race and a big cheer went up from the crowd.

Rachel and Kirsty were the last two
to hop over the finishing line, but they
were so happy they didn't mind a bit.

Then a special announcement came
over the tannoy. "We have some
good news: the medals and prize
certificates have just been found," came
a happy-sounding voice. "So everyone
will be able to collect them
before they go home!"

"Hurrah!" cheered all the children.

"It looks like the rest of Sports Day is going to be great fun now," Kirsty said happily.

"I think so, too," came a silvery voice from just behind her ear.

Kirsty and Rachel smiled at the little fairy who had reappeared beside them.

"Thanks, Tallulah," Rachel said. "Everyone's having a good time now."

"Well, I came to thank you for helping me," Tallulah replied.

"I'm off to spread my Tuesday magic
everywhere I can now. But before I go,
I just wanted to wish you luck in the
next race. Have you heard what it is?"

"No," Kirsty replied. "What?"

Tallulah smiled mysteriously. "I think
you'll like it," she laughed. "Goodbye
for now!" She waved her wand and
a swirl of turquoise sparkles tumbled
all around her. Then she was gone.

Before Kirsty or Rachel could say another word, another announcement began. "The next race will be the three-legged race," it said. "Would all competitors please line up at the starting line to have their legs tied."

Rachel and Kirsty burst out laughing. "We're definitely going to enter this one," Rachel said, grabbing Kirsty's hand.

Kirsty nodded. "We couldn't be any worse than the goblins!"

The Fun Day Fairies

Megan and Tallulah have got
their flags back. Now Rachel
and Kirsty must help

Willow the Wednesday Fairy

Win Rainbow Magic goodies!

In every book in the Rainbow Magic Fun Day Fairies series (books 36-42) there is a hidden picture of a flag with a secret letter in it. Find all seven letters and re-arrange them to make a special Fairyland word, then send it to us. Each month we will put the entries into a draw and select one winner to receive a Rainbow Magic Sparkly T-shirt and Goody Bag!

Send your entry on a postcard to Rainbow Magic Fun Day Competition, Orchard Books, 338 Euston Road, London NW1 3BH. Australian readers should write to Hachette Children's Books, Level 17/207 Kent Street, Sydney, NSW 2000. Don't forget to include your name and address. Only one entry per child. Final draw: 30th September 2007.

Have you checked out the

website at:
www.rainbowmagic.co.uk

RAINBOW magic ®

by Daisy Meadows

The Rainbow Fairies

The Weather Fairies

The Party Fairies

The Jewel Fairies

The Pet Keeper Fairies

Katie the Kitten Fairy	ISBN	1 84616 166 5
Bella the Bunny Fairy	ISBN	1 84616 170 3
Georgia the Guinea Pig Fairy	ISBN	1 84616 168 1
Lauren the Puppy Fairy	ISBN	1 84616 169 X
Harriet the Hamster Fairy	ISBN	1 84616 167 3
Molly the Goldfish Fairy	ISBN	1 84616 172 X
Penny the Pony Fairy	ISBN	1 84616 171 1

The Fun Day Fairies

Megan the Monday Fairy	ISBN	1 84616 188 6
Tallulah the Tuesday Fairy	ISBN	1 84616 189 4
Willow the Wednesday Fairy	ISBN	1 84616 190 8
Thea the Thursday Fairy	ISBN	1 84616 191 6
Freya the Friday Fairy	ISBN	1 84616 192 4
Sienna the Saturday Fairy	ISBN	1 84616 193 2
Sarah the Sunday Fairy	ISBN	1 84616 194 0

Holly the Christmas Fairy	ISBN	1 84362 661 6
Summer the Holiday Fairy	ISBN	1 84362 960 7
Stella the Star Fairy	ISBN	1 84362 869 4
Kylie the Carnival Fairy	ISBN	1 84616 175 4
The Rainbow Magic Treasury	ISBN	1 84616 047 2

Coming soon:

Paige the Pantomime Fairy	ISBN	1 84616 209 2

All priced at £3.99. *Holly the Christmas Fairy, Summer the Holiday Fairy,*
Stella the Star Fairy and *Kylie the Carnival Fairy* are priced at £5.99.
The Rainbow Magic Treasury is priced at £12.99.
Rainbow Magic books are available from all good bookshops, or can be ordered
direct from the publisher: Orchard Books, PO BOX 29, Douglas IM99 1BQ
Credit card orders please telephone 01624 836000
or fax 01624 837033 or visit our Internet site: www.wattspub.co.uk
or e-mail: bookshop@enterprise.net for details.

To order please quote title, author and ISBN and your full name and address.
Cheques and postal orders should be made payable to 'Bookpost plc.'
Postage and packing is FREE within the UK
(overseas customers should add £2.00 per book).
Prices and availability are subject to change.

Look out for the Petal Fairies!

TIA THE TULIP FAIRY
1-84616-457-5

PIPPA THE POPPY FAIRY
1-84616-458-3

LOUISE THE LILY FAIRY
1-84616-459-1

CHARLOTTE THE
SUNFLOWER FAIRY
1-84616-460-5

OLIVIA THE ORCHID FAIRY
1-84616-461-3

DANIELLE THE DAISY FAIRY
1-84616-462-1

ELLA THE ROSE FAIRY
1-84616-464-8

Available from
Thursday 5th April 2007